The Albawich Nightmare

By Akaash Hussain

Chapter One

Chloe left the bar after a night out with her friends. This was a common occurrence as her friends lived on the opposite side of town. She lived the closest so at the end of the night she would walk home as they sat at the bar waiting for their ride home to arrive. There were no taxis available in the area and the buses were no longer operating as it was nearly midnight. Chloe had no choice but to walk to her apartment. This was not an inconvenience to her as it was only a short ten-minute walk. After all, this would save her some money that she could use later on to order food to her apartment.

The parking prices in the city centre were extortionate. This was one of the reasons that Chloe did not like bringing her car to the city centre. But this time she wished that she had made an exception. As it started to rain heavily, causing Chloe's clothes to get drenched and her shoes began to fill with rainwater. She jogged through the city centre, passing by the shops as their shutters rattled due to the heavy winds. On the other side of the road there were people dressed in their fancy outfits, waiting eagerly to be let into the clubs and bars as they got drenched in the rain. To be fair, this was not their fault, the weather was forecast to be warm and dry. The weather that actually occurred could not have been any more opposite.

Under the bridge there was a hoard of homeless people. They gathered around a skip that was lit on fire. It provided them with much needed warmth, as the thunder roared, and the city got battered by buckets of rain. Chloe crossed the road, hopping over a small stream of water flowing across the middle of the road that had formed due to the bad weather. As she turned the corner, a drunk lady approached and asked Chloe if she had a lighter. Before spitting at her after she told the lady that she did not have one. Chloe avoided confrontation at all times, as she had a very civilised nature. She was taught martial arts by her late father when she was younger. And promised him that she would only ever strike somebody if her life were in danger. A promise that she would fulfil as her journey continued. Chloe kept her head down as she walked through a tunnel and passed by a group of young people, that were spraying graffiti art on the walls. The art was actually really impressive, maybe the young people were artists during the day. One could only hope that they would use their talent in a more rewarding way. Chloe then approached a set of stairs that led to a road opposite to the apartment block where she lived. Looking left and right for any joy riders. Being cautious was mandatory as there have been multiple accidents due to this road being one of the longest straight roads in the city without any speed cameras.

Chloe crossed the road and headed towards the entrance of the apartment building. She tried to type the entrance code to gain access, but there was no feedback. Nothing was happening. She tried entering the code another two times. Still nothing happened. It appeared to have been broken. So, she decided to push against the door, to her surprise it opened. Chloe smiled in relief, for a couple of seconds she was worried that she would have been locked out of the apartment in the bad weather. She walked up a set of stairs and could hear the sound of music blasting through one of the apartments on the second floor. As she walked towards it, there were a group of people stood outside the room holding plastic cups and appeared to be having a good time. As they laughed and joked with each other. It seemed to have been quite the party, as two people were passed out on the stairs.

Not the best situation to be in but they had their friends alongside so they must have been in safe hands. Well Chloe could only hope that this was the case, knowing that friends were sometimes just people you hung out with. Not all of them had your best interest at heart.

Chloe considered going to the party, before having second thoughts and made the wise decision not to go. She knew that this would lead to further drinking. And staying up late, it was already past midnight. She had already consumed a lot of alcohol when she was at the bar with her friends. She could just about walk in a straight line. Chloe passed by the room and walked up the stairs. The sound of music slowly faded away as she reached the fifth floor. She took a deep breath and smiled as she entered her apartment. She was relieved to finally be home. In warmth and comfort, away from aggressive drunk people. She took her shoes off and drained the rainwater out into the bathroom sink, leaving her shoes on top of the radiator. Hoping that they would dry by the morning. They were the only pair of shoes that she had. The only other footwear that she owned were heels. Not the best in this kind of weather.

Chloe opened her wardrobe and took out a pair of leggings and an oversized hoodie. She had bought these to wear at a sleep over with some of her childhood friends. But that was looking very unlikely to happen due to the drastic change in weather. Her belly started to rumble; this was because she had only had liquids to drink during the day as she did not have an appetite to eat. The food served at the bar was not to Chloe's hygiene standards. Chloe was never a picky or fussy person. This leaves little to imagination of how bad the food at the bar actually was. But now she was hungry.

So, she took her phone out of the handbag and ordered some pizza with a portion of chips from a food app on her phone. She had a free delivery promotion and fifty percent off from her meal. This was very ideal because Chloe was currently saving up to move into a new apartment. She made a promise to herself that she would cut down the amount of time that she ordered food to the apartment. Chloe changed into the leggings and oversized hoodie. The order arrived not long after. Chloe collected the order from outside her apartment and sat on the edge of the bed, eating two slices of pizza. The cheese was stretchy, and the chicken tikka and minced beef toppings were still sizzling. The pizza was fresh out of the oven, just how Chloe liked it. The chips on the other hand were soggy and moist. They must have got wet in the extreme weather outside. After eating the two slices she was feeling stuffed. Maybe because she had not eaten in such a long time. Chloe laid back and passed out from exhaustion. The rest was much needed, especially for the road ahead. This she would soon come to know.

A few hours later. Chloe was laying down staring at the ceiling fan, motionless. As the grandfather clock in the hallway ticked away. Every few seconds a gentle splash could be heard coming from the sink in the bathroom. And the sound would completely fade into the abyss, as the bass from the music at another party a couple of doors away shook the furniture. Chloe sat up and noticed that the pizza had fallen onto the floor, she must have knocked it over when she passed out. Still not fully awake, Chloe rolled out of bed and lifted the apartment window. As she smoked a cigarette whilst leaning forward onto the windowsill.

There was not much of a view to enjoy. Even though her apartment was on the fifth floor. This was the highest floor in the building. All Chloe could see was the occasional glimpse of creepy shadow figures in the dark alleyway, at the front of the apartment building. Caused by the flashes of lightning. The thunder roared in the sky as the heavy rain put out Chloe's cigarette. After all, nature was in full effect.

The old window had seen better days. As the wood on the edges had expanded over time. So, Chloe had to drag the window down in order for it to shut properly. The maintenance guy was supposed to come and replace the window two nights earlier but had to cancel due to the bad weather. He said that he could not replace it until the weather had settled. This was understandable. But it was not understandable that no other maintenance people lived in the area. As though they were going extinct. Chloe picked up the pizza box and threw it into the bin as she walked across the hallway to enter the outdated bathroom. The bathroom looked like it was ripped straight out of a Rob Zombie movie. A cold shiver travelled through her spine as it was very cold. The walls were covered in mould. Even the discoloured wallpaper was hanging off from different parts of the wall. It was the perfect setting for somebody to smash through the door with an axe and shout *'Here's Johnny!'*

Chloe splashed her face with cold water causing her to fully wake up. She decided to brush her teeth because she did not get a chance to do this before she fell asleep. It was a battle squeezing the last few blobs of toothpaste from the tube. She started to rinse her mouth, when all of a sudden, she could feel the sensation of something tapping her shoulder. She quickly turned around and a cockroach fell from her shoulder into the sink. She watched the creature crawl into a hole inside the wall on the side of the sink. This made Chloe go into deep thoughts. About how nice it would be to move into a new apartment, this felt good but seemed too far from becoming a reality.

She used to live in an amazing apartment that was fully furnished and equipped with the best of things. Once you have had a taste of that life. It is hard to have to settle for less. The apartment Chloe used to live in belonged to her ex-boyfriend. Having an amazing apartment like that was just a dream. Until her phone began to ring. *Sorry to bother you at this time Chloe. I need you down at Albawich as soon as possible to cover a story. It is breaking news material and I will give you a bonus cheque after you cover the story. I will text you the coordinates.* Said Harvey.

Harvey was a successful business owner. The CEO of a news company called Albawich Today. He was middle aged and single. Harvey was very career focused and believed that being in a relationship with someone would be a huge distraction. He was a very humble and down to earth individual. Anybody that did not know him, would not be able to tell that he was the CEO of a very successful company. Over the years he had proven to be very resourceful as he published news articles and live television reports at least 12 hours before any other media outlet in the area. His reputation and credibility were built on these foundations. He would also pay people good money in the area for genuine news. He was the only news company in Albawich that operated this way. Using a pay to win strategy to gain the edge on his competitors. Making his company the leading news company that it is today.

Throughout Chloe's career as a news reporter, she craved a breakthrough story that would catapult her career and lifestyle to another level. Everything that she had always wished for was now in her reach. The dream of living in a new apartment was now a lot closer to becoming a reality. This was truly a life changing moment for her. Little did she know, the journey ahead was full of surprises. The kind of surprises that one does not wish to be involved in. *I am on my way. Send the location.* Chloe replied before quickly getting changed into a shirt and a pencil skirt.

She always kept a pair of professional clothes ready just in case she had to drop everything and leave. Like she had to at this very moment. Going down the stairs was not an option, as Chloe's apartment was situated on the fifth floor, and she was wearing high heals. Her other pair of shoes were still wet from the journey home after the night out with friends in the city centre. And the rest of her heels were reserved for posh dates and conferences. They were too expensive to wear out in such weather. Chloe took her car keys from the bedside cabinet. She looked in the mirror and fixed her hair, then exited the apartment and locked the door behind her as she walked down the hallway.

Chapter Two

Chloe walked to the elevator down the hallway, pressing the button and waiting for the elevator to arrive patiently. She kept one hand on the wall to maintain her balance, as the bass coming from the music in one of the apartments was causing her heels to vibrate. Giving her trouble staying balanced. It was almost like being drunk, walking in a straight line without extra help was not possible. The elevator was directly across from the room, this made the effects of the base more intense. The elevator doors opened, and Chloe stepped in. The doors closed instantly banishing the sounds of music and putting a halt to the vibration.

The elevator went down to the underground garage. As Chloe exited the elevator she was met by an eerie silence. The feeling of being watched overcame her. The only thing that she could hear was the sound of her heals tapping down on the ground causing loud echoes. She panicked and sped up until she was nearly jogging while looking around, in an attempt to shake the eerie feeling.

Chloe got into the car, slamming the door shut and quickly pressing the button to lock all the doors. She now felt safe as the feeling of being watched slowly wore off. She switched on the ignition. Connecting her phone's Bluetooth to the car after typing the location sent by her boss. As Chloe drove out of the underground garage, the silence was met by a burst of pouring rain coupled with thunder and lightning. She turned the radio on, to mask the sounds of heavy winds battering the car from outside. The signal on the radio was unbearable due to the weather. *I guess I will just have to listen to nature's live rock concert then.* Chloe said to herself in a disappointed tone. The windscreen wiper was on the fastest setting. But this made no difference. The visibility was so bad that the view from the windscreen was as though Chloe was blinking as fast as she possibly could.

Needless to mention, these conditions were almost guaranteed to lead to a disaster.

The GPS signal cut out as Chloe drove down the long stretch of road that led to the small town of Albawich. The navigation display started flickering. Tapping the top of the display did not help matters as this caused the display to black out entirely. This all happened on the worst part of the journey. A dark unlit road with nobody around. She then turned her attention towards the road in front of her, causing her to slam the brakes. But at this point it was too late.

The heavy downpour of rain caused a dip in the road to become heavily flooded. Things seemed to start going down hill from here on. The front part of the car was under water, the car's power immediately cut out as well. Luckily, Chloe climbed into the back of the car and kicked through one of the windows, escaping just in time. As the flood relentlessly swallowed the car. Her mobile phone perished the same fate as her car. She knew that she had to find shelter expeditiously as she was in the middle of nowhere. And the weather was not looking to calm any time soon. With the road blocked off by a huge flood, she had to find another route to get into Albawich.

Chloe noticed that there was a narrow path on the side of the road that lead into the woods. It looked dangerous and creepy. With no signs of life as far as her eyes could see, this was the only option. She did not have the luxury to stand on the side of the road in hopes of being rescued. Chloe took her heals off and left them on side of the road. *I cannot walk through the swamp wearing these. Luckily, I did not wear the expensive pair. Ewe gross.* Chloe complained in disgust as her feet sank into the wet mud that oozed between her toes.

If anybody saw the manner in which she was walking they would have thought that she was possessed by a demon. After a couple of minutes of walking, Chloe looked back and could not see anything. It was as though everything had rendered into darkness. It was frightening to look around as the constant lightning cast many creepy shadows from the trees. She then heard some twigs snap to her side as if someone had stepped on them.

This caught her attention and to her horror, the sound came from the direction of a gravestone. *What the hell is a gravestone doing in the middle of the woods?* Chloe screamed as she picked up pace and started to run. This was a bad idea as she slipped and fell and slid to the bottom of the path. Luckily, she only had minor scrapes to her legs. To her comfort she could now see a light in the distance. The closer she got, the clearer she could see that the light was coming from a house. She headed towards it in hopes to get help and most importantly, shelter. She began to overthink. The aesthetics of the house were not helping with her thoughts. *Why would somebody live in the middle of the woodland? I've seen 'The Hills Have Eyes' too many times to know better. Oh well I am here now.* Chloe whispered to herself.

Chapter Three

Chloe approached the creepy old house hesitantly as there was a huge signpost in front of it that stated 'NO TRESPASSING. TRESSPASSERS WILL BE SHOT'. *Maybe this was a bad idea I should head back and wait for help.* Said Chloe as she turned back until she heard another few twigs snap and the sound of howling coming from the distance. She could see something stood on the path where she came from, but it was too far for her to see more than just a creepy silhouette. She could see enough to know that there was most definitely something stood there. It was clearly too dangerous to head back.

Chloe had to take her chances, so she braved her way to the front porch of the house. In front of her was a huge door as she stood face to face with an old rusty door knocker. She used it to knock the door six times. There was no answer. She knocked six more times. Still no response. After knocking another six times, she decided to walk around the house and look through the windows to see if she could see anybody. There was nothing but darkness. It was like she was trying to look through limousine tint windows. The house appeared quiet and empty. Chloe turned the door handle and the door creaked wide open. *Hello, is anybody home? My car broke down and I was wondering if I could use a phone to call for help. I promise that I am not trespassing, Hello.* Called out Chloe before entering the house after nobody responded to her. She had no choice but to let herself in.

She entered the house. Leaving a trail of muddy footprints on the porch behind her. She was too anxious to notice this. *Hello is anybody home?* There was no response. She closed the front door and entered the lounge. She was welcomed into the room by a damp rotting smell. As a swarm of flies flew away from what looked like a bowl of fish guts. The old, stained settee had ripped fabric hanging down from the arm rests. A lightbulb hung from an exposed wire in the ceiling. Sat in front of the old-fashioned television was a wooden rocking chair, next to an old table covered in newspapers that were held down by an ashtray that contributed to the overall smell of the room. The walls fitted in with the rest of the theme in the lounge, as they were covered in mould and cockroaches weaved through the tears in the wallpaper. Chloe quickly stepped out of the lounge and walked into the kitchen.

There was a pile of disposable plates and cups covered in mould as rats nibbled away at the remains of whatever food was eaten in them. She looked out of the kitchen window and could see that the house was overlooking a river that flowed in front of a graveyard. *If there is a graveyard over there, then why was there a gravestone out in the woodland?* Chloe asked herself. Staring closely at the mist that was surrounding the graveyard. She could see something with white glowing eyes staring directly at her from behind one of the gravestones.

The thing slowly stood up from behind the gravestone. It stood at a frightening height of around 8 feet tall. Chloe screamed in terror and stumbled backwards, then ran through the lounge leading to the wooden staircase. She panicked as all she could see in her mind were flashbacks of when the tall white eyed lady stared directly at her from the graveyard. She slowly walked up the staircase.

As she reached the top of the staircase, she knocked on a bedroom door. *Hello is anybody home?* Asked Chloe. Once again, she did not get any response. At this point she was absolutely convinced that nobody was home. When she entered the other bedroom, she could hear the sound of a vehicle approaching the house from a distance. Only a few seconds later the tyres screeched as the truck pulled up outside of the house. Afraid that she would get shot for trespassing, Chloe hid in one of the rooms upstairs. Then carefully peeked out from the corner of the window and could see the back of a creepy looking old man. He was dragging something out from the back of his truck. And dragged it towards a well in the distance. It was too dark to see exactly what he was dragging. This made Chloe's imagination run wild. As there was a dark red trail following whatever the creepy old man was dragging. The lightning flashed and caused everything to momentarily light up. To her shock she saw that the old man was dragging a body bag. He lifted it over his shoulder and threw it into the well.

Upon closer observation, the supposed well was actually a huge underground fire pit as sparks of fire hovered above it. The creepy old man turned around. Chloe quickly hid below the window. After catching a glimpse of the old man's disfigured face. His eyes were bloodshot red and wide open as though they were being held open by a pair of matchsticks. His jaw was bent painfully to the left and his neck slanted to the left as well. Her prior worries had become a reality. It was like she had walked onto the set of 'The Hills Have Eyes'. Chloe carefully peeked out from the corner of the window again. The old man was walking back to his truck almost like he had forgotten something.

He reached into a bucket and pulled out a decapitated head dripping with blood. Chloe fell back in shock as she gasped for air. She laid there in disbelief of what she had just witnessed. What made this worse was that Chloe recognised the head, it belonged to a well-known local priest named Father Lucas. Father Lucas was a close friend of Chloe's late father. She had countless memories of him joining her family at the dinner table. The last time she had spoken to him, they spoke about the importance of living a life that was one of purpose.

Surely Father Lucas had fulfilled a life of purpose. A man like that deserved to pass away in peace. Not to be murdered in such a brutal manner. The look of fright was all over his face, indicating that he was pretty much alert in his final moments. Chloe reluctantly peeked out of the window again but this time she was shaking in fear. The old man threw the decapitated head into the fire pit and dragged a metal cover over it. Chloe quickly hid once again to avoid getting seen by the creepy old man. *This cannot be real; how can this be real?* Chloe asked herself in disbelief after what she had just witnessed.

The creepy old man reached into the truck and switched the engine off. Then slammed the door shut and started walking towards the house. As he approached the house, muddy footprints on the porch caught his attention. This made him very angry. Being the kind of person that does not ever have any guests over at his house. The night of Halloween being an exception.

He rushed into the house and took a rifle from above the coat hanger. Then he walked through the front room aiming through the sights of the rifle. Walking through to the kitchen, he opened the back door and looked for footprints leading away from the house. He then knew that whoever had entered his house, did not leave. The creepy old man clearly had a lot of experience hunting people. Chloe hid inside the laundry basket, in the bathroom and covered herself in the creepy old man's dirty clothes. This put him to the test as the game of hide and seek commenced.

Loud footsteps could be heard as the creepy old man walked up the staircase. Scraping his rifle across the wall. He knew that somebody was still inside the house as there were only footprints facing in the direction of the house on the porch and no footprints leading away from the house. The creepy old man once again looked down the barrel of his rifle before stepping into one of the bedrooms. Using the tip of the rifle, the old man rifled through the wardrobe and then knelt down to check under the bed. Chloe was still in the laundry basket trying to stay as still and quiet as possible. When the man stepped into the bathroom, he looked behind the shower curtain. Then turned around, totally ignoring the laundry basket and heading back downstairs. But things were far from over.

Chloe saw this as an opportunity to climb out of the dirty laundry basket and hide in one of the rooms that the creepy old man had already checked. Thinking that he would not check the same place twice. The creepy old man walked out of the front door and headed in the direction of a shed. Chloe peeked out of the corner of the window to see where he was going. She was wishful thinking that he would just get into his car and drive away fading into the darkness.

Sadly, in reality things rarely turn out how one would expect them to. This was confirmed when she saw the creepy old man drag a huge roll of barbed wire towards the house. He dragged it upstairs. Chloe stood still in the cupboard feeling puzzled until, the creepy old man slowly started to lay the barbed wire all over the landing upstairs. The game of hide and seek was becoming a scene from one of the 'Saw' movies.

He then covered the staircase with barbed wire as well. The floorboards jolted as he bolted the barbed wire down to the floor with a nail gun. He knew that the person in his house was bare foot, based on the footprints that lead into the house. This went one step further as the creepy old man carried a huge box of broken glass from the shed into the house. Scattering it all over the landing upstairs and on the staircase. Chloe panicked as the sound of footsteps faded and were replaced by the sound of rocking. The creepy old man was sat on the rocking chair in the lounge. Rocking back and forth, he waited eagerly as this was now a waiting game. *I know you are in the house, make your whereabouts be known. If I have to come upstairs, I swear to Lucifer, I will drag your body through the glass and barbed wire. And watch you bathe in the river of piranhas!* Shouted the creepy old man.

The details of the creepy old man's threat were very unsettling. Chloe did not know what to do. She only knew that she could not stay hidden forever. She sneaked to the window; it was at the back of the house overlooking the graveyard. Where Chloe saw the white eyed lady. Only this time the white eyed lady was standing closer to the house. As though she had swum across the river. This was enough to cause Chloe to sneak into one of the rooms that overlooked the front of the house. Before she could do that, she had to figure out a way across the glass and barbed wire on the landing. She had to think outside the box. She decided to place a footstool between both rooms So that she could use it to step on and jump over to the other room.

She timed this with the rocking sound of the rocking chair. After executing her plan successfully, she gained access to the room that overlooked the front of the house. Chloe was faced with another task. She realised that in order for her to get to the opening, she would have to drag something to the window to gain the extra height required to open it.

The windows in this house were extraordinarily tall. It would not be a surprise if the tall lady from behind the gravestone lived here. Reaching the window would be tricky, as the creepy old man was sat on the rocking chair directly below the room. Alerting him of her presence would most certainly have grave consequences. The way in which he set up the traps and disposed of Father Lucas's brutalised body. It was clear that the creepy old man was not to be underestimated.

Chapter Four

The sound rocking stopped as the sound of a car approaching the house made both, Chloe and the creepy old man peek out of the window simultaneously. Blue and red flashing lights came closer as a police car pulled over beside the truck. Two police officers stepped out of the car. One of them had a flashlight. Chloe was in a dilemma, whether or not to alert them that she was in danger. Because she knew that the creepy old man was capable of murder. And could kill them if he felt like he needed to.

The police officers approached the porch. There was a knock on the door. *Can I help you?* Shouted the creepy old man as he opened the door ever so slightly. So that the police officers could not see the barbed wire and glass on the staircase. *We have had reports of a huge disturbance in the Albawich woodland, it had to be taped off due to the nature of what we found. We are out here asking locals if they have heard anything.* Responded the police officer. *I will be sure to let you know if I hear something officer.* Said the creepy old man.

The police officers turned around and walked towards their car until they noticed the dark red blood stains leading to the underground fire pit. The creepy old man was no longer in the house. He was slowly creeping up behind the two police officers. Oblivious to the view behind him, of Chloe climbing out of the window upstairs. She carefully walked along the ledge trying her best to keep her balance. The rain made it quite slippery up there.

Meanwhile, the police officers removed the metal cover from the fire pit. Before they could even look inside, they were approached by the creepy old man as he pushed them into the fire pit. The creepy old man leaned over and stared at the soon to be lifeless bodies of the police officers. As they ricochet from the walls, until they met their horrific demise. The previous ashes of the burnt corpses shot up into the sky. There was the sound of a sudden loud bang coming from the direction of the house. Catching the attention of the creepy old man, as Chloe jumped onto his truck to break her fall. Luckily, her pencil skirt ripped from the side, enabling her to make a quick get away. As a shot from the creepy old man's rifle whistled past her head and hit the fuel area of the police car. She escaped into the Albawich woodland. And the police car burst into flames.

Chloe ran through the woodland without looking back. Getting away from the creepy old man was the only thing on her mind as her feet splashed through the wet mud. The thunder, heavy rain and lightning were no longer a worry of hers. She took cover behind a fallen down tree to catch a breath and recompose herself. It was too creepy and dark for her to stay sat around too long. She then ran a lot further into the woodland.

Approaching the part of the woodland that was taped off by the police. There was nobody in sight, only blood and dead bodies covered in white sheets. Stunned by what she was witnessing, Chloe jumped in agony as she stepped on the ashes of a pentagram that had been burnt into the ground. Her foot sizzled as she put it back on the wet ground. Confused to why the pentagram was still warm despite the heavy rain. Chloe turned her attention to a well and could then hear chanting in a female's voice getting louder and louder.

She could see a tall lady in the distance. As she approached her, she called out. *Excuse me I need your help*. The tall lady turned around and Chloe fell to the ground screaming as this was the lady that was staring at her from behind the gravestone in the graveyard. The white eyed lady started pacing towards Chloe. Once she had processed in her mind what she was looking at, she crawled backwards and away from the white eyed lady.

Chloe got up from the ground and ran in the direction of a main road nearby. The white eyed lady stopped following her. One of the houses was flooded with reporters and hoards of people stood watching from behind the crime scene tape that blocked off the road. Through the heavy rain and thunder she could not quite make out what the news reporters were saying. Before she could ask anything, the locals started to speak amongst themselves and one of them could be heard saying. *They found Gareth's body but could not find his head. I heard that the witch that roams the woodland attacked him.* Chloe did not want to hear anymore, as it was freaking her out, she continued walking up the road. Even though Chloe did not live far from Albawich, she still had never visited the small town.

She could hear some twigs snapping to her side. She looked in the direction of where the sound came from and could see the shadow of something approaching her, she gasped in terror. As she was approached by a junkie. *Fear not, I come to warn not harm. These woods will eat your soul, not leaving Albawich will cost you more than a leg and an arm. You must leave Albawich. Before you get thrown into the well by the white eyed witch. He will eat your heart and your liver. You will be a meal for Lucifer. Jasper's bullet was meant to miss miss miss, because you are the target of six six six.* Chanted the junkie. *Get away from me you creep!* Shouted Chloe before running away from the junkie. *You may run from me, but Satan has already cast his eyes on thee. Leave this town and you will be free. Stay here and you will pay a fee. It will cost you dearly, this you will see.* Chanted the junkie. As Chloe ran into the distance. Ever since she stepped foot in Albawich she has been plagued with misfortune.

Chapter Five

The creepy old man sprayed fire extinguisher on to the flames of the burning police car. Surrounding the car in a white powdery mist momentarily. He waved his hands in front of himself to clear the mist from his view. It was too dangerous for him to leave the car in plain sight. This could lead to the countless bodies being found in the fire pit and not to mention, the endless number of corpses buried on the very land that the house was built on. Too much to lose, the creepy old man towed the police car to the back of his truck. And drove around 200 feet away from the house. Dragging the junk along the path. To a very tall tree in the woodland.

The tree must have been over one hundred years old as it stood strong amongst the other trees. This tree looked like it had witnessed some frightening horrors over the decades. It aged very badly and looked like something from 'Resident Evil'. The creepy old man detached the hook from his truck and began to climb the tree. Surprisingly with ease he got to the top. He must have done this before. He knew exactly where to put his feet and knew exactly where to reach. He threw the hook over a couple of strong branches then climbed back down to the ground almost as easily as he climbed the tree.

He jumped up to reach the hook that was dangling down from the tree above and then reattached it to the back of his truck. The creepy old man then drove the truck forward and suddenly the police car vanished. It disappeared as it lifted into the tree and hid under the leaves like a present under a Christmas tree. But never to be found. Not any time soon it would seem. He stepped out of the truck to admire his work. As he looked up, he could not see the car.

This was great, if the creepy old man could not see the car, then this meant that no passers by would see the car. A crow flew across the sky and sat on top of some of the wreckage on top of the tree. Amongst many other wreckages. There were multiple wheelchairs, cars and even a bus that had been lifted into the tree. The amounts of rust on the wreckage explained the colour of the tree as it must have leaked down onto it consistently over the decades.

After detaching the hook and reeling the chain into the back of his truck, the creepy old man drove back towards the house. He was in a dilemma whether or not to pursue his unwelcome guest. The decision he needed to make was soon clear to him. Upon approaching the house, he could see something in the distance shining on the ground near where he last saw Chloe. He parked up besides it and got out of the car. Kneeling down to the ground, he picked up a business card belonging to Chloe.

The occupation was listed as 'News Reporter'. Things now got a lot worse for him as he tied up one loose end only to find out that another one got loose. Now knowing the identity of the mystery woman, he had to think fast. Piecing everything together he gathered that she could only be heading to one place. The scene of the crime that the police officers were talking about. There could be a lot of people and news companies there. Fearing that his secrets could be uncovered. The creepy old man loaded the rifle with new bullets and spun the truck around before heading towards the residential area of Albawich.

Drained of energy and suffering from dehydration. Chloe was exhausted and in shock from what she had just experienced. She wished that she had missed Harvey's call so she would not have been caught up in the middle of a horror movie. Her desire to change her life is what drove her to Albawich. Which it did. It changed her life. But not in the way that she expected it. The phrase 'Be careful what you wish for' was very relevant at this moment. Chloe needed a miracle as she walked slowly along the road across from the Albawich woodland when a vehicle started approaching from behind her. She was unaware of this due to the sound of heavy winds battering the trees in the woodland. And the sound of rain smacking against the tarmac on the road.

Chloe noticed a vehicle pulled over besides her. Causing her to jump in fright. Thinking that the creepy old man had caught up with her. *Chloe, is that you? What the hell happened? I have been trying to contact you. Where have you been? And why are you covered in mud? Come on get in.* Asked a very concerned Harvey as he leant over to open the passenger door for her to get in. Chloe got into the car and hugged Harvey as she was relieved to feel a sense of security and safety. *I hope you got some popcorn because I have got a headlining story for you.* Chloe then went on to explain what happened from the time her car broke down.

All of the people at the crime scene alongside the reporters stood in silence as they stared at the creepy old man drive past them. They were all shook to the core. The fear in their eyes, only made the creepy old man feel empowered. This was a feeling he was not used to. As he lived away from the general public, isolated by all things that lurked in the woodland. He drove slowly, turning his head only to stare into the eyes of everybody one by one. They stood frozen in fear as he passed by them. He drove his truck up the road before having to slam his brakes. Stood in front of the car was the junkie. *Curse you Jasper! Leave that lady alone! Rotten you are from flesh to bone.* Shouted the Junkie. *Go away Or I will kill you for good this time Rebecca.* Responded Jasper before driving around the junkie and continuing up the road.

Chloe had filled Harvey in on her experiences leading up until he found her. *By the sounds of what you are telling me Chloe. This man that you speak of, Is Jasper. He was forced out of the residential area in Albawich some thirty years ago. Since then, he has rarely ever been seen. People from neighbouring towns would go missing. There were rumours that Jasper was abducting people and scattering their remains in the land within*

22

the woods. Police could not do anything as they had no proof of this. Jasper himself blamed it all on some serial killer that terrorised the town of Albawich during the eighteen hundreds. Nobody believed him as that was around two hundred years ago. Explained Harvey. *Do you believe him?* Asked Chloe. *You know that I do not rule things out very easily, there is more credibility to the sighting of a so called white eyed witch that roams the woodland at witching hour ever so often.* Answered Harvey as he pulled into the driveway of his house. *I was not expecting visitors today so mind the mess. And I hope you are hungry because I have got quite a lot of food stocked up. I do not usually stockpile but with the weather we have been getting lately, it is better to be on the safe side. There should be everything you need upstairs. Give me a shout if you need anything. I will cook something tasty in the meantime.* Said Harvey. As he made his way to the kitchen.

Chapter Six

Chloe walked up the stairs and saw that some clothes were hung on the radiator. She walked over to them and touched them. They were dry so she took a t-shirt and a pair of sweatpants before entering the bathroom. She switched the light on and was amazed by the modern feel of the bathroom. The last time she was in a modern and well-designed bathroom was when she lived with her ex-boyfriend. She was stepped into the shower and switched it on then sat on the toilet seat as she waited for the room to fill with steam.

Chloe was glad that she was rescued by Harvey. It was too dangerous for her to be wondering outside. Especially when there had been multiple murders and two crime scenes. And even worse, a creepy old man armed with a rifle. She was safe indoors. In the company of somebody that she knew and trusted. At least this is what she thought.

The room was now full of steam like a sauna. Chloe removed her clothes and put them in the bin. *There is no way that I am wearing those again.* Said Chloe, knowing that the clothes would be a constant reminder of her frightening near death experience. She then stepped into the shower cubicle as the water washed away the mud from her body. Only to reveal bloody scratches on her legs and feet. This must have happened when she was running aimlessly through the Albawich woodland.

She could feel a sharp pain coming from her back. She looked at her back in the mirror and the letters '666' were scratched onto it. She had no idea when that could have happened. Her imagination went wild. *Could there have been any truth to what that creepy lady was saying about the devil, or does this have something to do with the white eyed lady?* Chloe asked herself as she stood confused. Downstairs, Harvey cooked fish fingers and fries.

Chloe stepped out of the shower and dried herself down with a towel before getting clothed. The '666' scratches were no longer on her back. Maybe it was just her eyes playing tricks on her. She hoped, unfortunately everything was very real. The white eyed lady, Jasper and the junkie were not the result of her eyes playing tricks on her. She went straight to the window at the end of the hallway, overlooking the road in front of the house. All she could see was heavy rain pouring down the road and trees shaking violently.

Chloe smiled as she felt that she had the perfect story that would make the front page in all of the newspapers. The recognition that she had always craved. A story much bigger than the one that she had embarked on the journey towards. She snapped out of her thoughts as her belly rumbled in hunger. The smell of fish fingers and fries made her think back to the time her late father used to bring her home from school. Fish fingers and fries were her favourite. Her dad used to cook them for her while she sat watching cartoons on the television. This made her feel at home.

Chloe made her way down the stairs and joined Harvey at the dining table. They both ate whilst watching a live news broadcast on the television. *I have decided that I am going to reveal to the public, information about what I witnessed at the creepy old man's house.* Chloe told Harvey. *Chloe that is very brave of you and I support you one hundred percent. We will get to it first thing in the morning.* Responded Harvey. It was getting late so Chloe took the dishes to the sink. Then immediately the feeling of dread came over her. Feeling as though something was staring at her from outside.

Something ran past the window nearly giving Chloe a heart attack. Wondering in the garden was a fox. Chloe shook her head in embarrassment and switched off the kitchen light before heading up the stairs. Meanwhile Harvey fell asleep on a sofa in the lounge. Chloe walked up the staircase carefully so that she would not wake up Harvey. It had been an eventful day. Chloe had met many characters. Some of which she did not intend on getting involved with.

Chloe laid down in bed and switched the table lamp off. The moonlight shined through the window. The shadows from the trees cast creepy shadows on the bedroom wall. She slowly drifted off into sleep. She began to dream; she had just got the keys to her new apartment. The sort of apartment that she had always wanted to have. Full of excitement she opened the door and stepped into one of the rooms in Jasper's house. She relived the moment that she saw Jasper drag the body of Father Lucas from his truck. Her dream had now become a nightmare. She then heard the sound of somebody calling for help.

This was weird as this was not how the events unfolded. Chloe woke up and could hear the same sound from her dream. But this time while she was awake. *Help! Help! Somebody help!* Chloe heard the cries for help coming from a distance. She climbed out of bed, then stared outside the window. She could see nothing. So, she gently walked downstairs trying her best not to wake up Harvey. As he snored on the sofa. She opened the front door and walked down the driveway, crossing over to the woodland. This was where the sounds of cries for help were coming from. She followed the sound that led very deep into to woodland. She knew that this was not the best thing to do but her kind heart made it impossible for her to ignore. The cries for help suddenly stopped. The area looked familiar to Chloe.

A feeling of terror came over Chloe as she was staring at the same gravestone in the middle of the woods that she saw earlier in the night. It was carved 'Rebecca 1826 – 1894'. Chloe could hear footsteps coming in her direction and the feeling of dread came over her again. Her legs trembled in fear as she ran all of the way back to Harvey's house not looking back even once. She was so scared that the run home took longer than it should have. It was like she was running in a nightmare. The path seemed to get longer and longer. Even though it took her longer to get home. She had gotten home just in time to escape the eyes of Jasper as his car turned into the road, just seconds after Chloe had gotten home.

Jasper drove down the road staring at the houses. After having no luck locating Chloe on the streets. He knew that most of the locals were at the crime scene. This meant that Chloe could be in one of the houses that had the lights switched on. There were only three houses that fit Jasper's criteria. Before he could go and investigate the houses, he was approached by a police car. The car pulled over besides his truck.

A little far out from your house Jasper, have not seen you out in this part of Albawich before, what brings you here? Asked the policewoman. *I heard of the incident in the woodland, so I thought I would come and have a sniff.* Responded Jasper. *Have you heard of the saying, all that comes to a sniffing man is trouble?* Asked the policewoman. *I will be on my way home officer.* Responded Jasper as he took the "saying" as a warning to leave. As much as Jasper wished that this encounter with the police officer was in the woodland, this was not the case. Jasper put his handbrake down and gently pulled away from the police car. Leaving the residential area of Albawich. And headed back to his house in the woodland. Until he could come up with another plan to silence Chloe.

The following morning, Chloe was woken by Harvey. As he rushed into her room. *Chloe quick there has been another incident, I want us to cover this one and you can report it. The news crew are already at the scene. They are waiting for you.* Said Harvey as he gave her one of his shirts and a long trench coat to wear. Chloe quickly got ready and headed out with Harvey as he reversed out of the driveway and sped off to the scene of the incident. Meanwhile, Jasper had a restless night. He was up all night obsessed with finding the whereabouts of Chloe. His obsession to find her lead him to search a directory book that listed a company called 'Albawich Today'. This was the company name displayed on

Chloe's identification card that he found the night earlier. The address registered to Albawich Today was a house in the residential area of Albawich under the name of Harvey Adams, listed as the director of the company.

Jasper filled with excitement as now knew the whereabouts of Chloe. And knew that he had to prepare for a man called Harvey as well. It was not often that Jasper got to brutally murder an accomplished person. There were not many successful people in Albawich. And the ones that were, knew to stay the hell out of evils way. But Harvey on the other hand was now also a target of Jasper. He looked forward to the challenge as he got into his truck and revved the engine before launching his car through the path, and onto the main road. The road that leads to Albawich.

Chapter Seven

Chloe and Harvey arrived at the scene of the incident. Chloe got out of the car and rushed to the news crew to prepare the news report. And get the mic attached to her. Harvey approached the young couple that reported the incident. *Hi my name's Harvey. I believe it was you guys that reported this incident to my news company?* Harvey asked the young couple. *Yes, we were going on our early morning walk, and we saw three vultures fly past us. It startled us as we were not expecting to see vultures in a small town like this. When we got closer, we saw the car and the man that I am guessing was being fed on by the vultures.* The young man told Harvey. *We appreciate you informing us of this immediately. Here take this money and treat your Mrs to something nice.* Laughed Harvey in an attempt to cheer the young couple's mood. He handed the young man two hundred pounds. As a thank you. The young couple left the scene.

Chloe had just gone live on air. *A man known locally as Justin has been found dead in a car wreck, two locals have said that they were on a walk when they discovered the car wreck with Justin's lifeless body inside. For more updates, please stay tuned. Chloe Slater, Albawich Today.* Chloe signed out before heading towards Harvey. He was attempting to have a civil conversation with Rebecca, the junkie that Chloe had encountered the night before. This was the lady that belonged to the grave. The grave that Chloe had seen when she ventured out into the woodland, following the deceptive screams for help.

The witches and ghosts dictate the outcome of one's destiny despite the popular belief that it has already been written. Said Rebecca. The news crew and Chloe looked at each other in confusion, they did not know what Rebecca was talking about. Neither did Harvey. So he walked away from her and headed towards the car where Chloe waited for him. They got into the car. *Harvey that lady do you know her?* Asked Chloe. *No, I have never seen her before, she looked like she had been dead for a hundred years.* Responded Harvey. *That is because she has been dead for over a hundred years!* Shouted Chloe as Harvey looked at her in confusion. *Her grave is in the middle of the woods I saw it with my own eyes.* Said Chloe. *What? The gravestone that you saw moments after your car got stranded?* Asked Harvey. *Yes, that is the one, Harvey something is not right, I can feel it. We need to leave Albawich.* Pleaded Chloe.

We cannot just pack our bags and leave just because you have a bad feeling. I live here, generations of my family have lived here. I have built my reputation here. I worked day and night until I gave my soul to the company. Said Harvey. Considering all the things that had happened lately, this was a creepy thing for Harvey to say. But Chloe did not pick up on it. Instead, her mind was racing as she sensed danger.

They headed to the local cafe for breakfast as they missed breakfast in the morning. In order to be the first media company to report the incident. Upon arriving, there was a 'Closed' sign on the door. Harvey rolled down his window and asked a passer by if he knew why the cafe was closed. *Did you not hear, the lady that worked here was brutally murdered last night?* Asked the passer by. *Another murder? What the hell is going on?* Harvey asked himself in shock. Before turning the car around and heading home so that Chloe could write the headline detailing the incident she was involved in the night before. *I know you are upset Chloe. You have been through a lot. I will tell you what. Once you have written your article, we will publish it and I will fly us out somewhere nice. Seeing you like this worries me.* Said Harvey as he offered Chloe some words of comfort.

As they approached the house, they were waved down by a local man. Harvey pulled over. *Can I help you sir?* Asked Harvey. *Do you have any guests over at your house?* Asked the local man. *Haha yes, I do, and her name is Chloe.* Laughed Harvey. *No, I am talking about the old man.* Said the local. As Chloe and Harvey looked at each other in shock. They knew that the person that the local man was talking about could only have been Jasper, the creepy old man. Harvey put his foot on the pedal and sped in the direction of his house. *Harvey stop! He will kill us; I have seen what he is capable of!* Shouted Chloe. *He is in my house how dare he enter my house; he has crossed the line. Watch what happens when I get a hold of him!* Shouted Harvey as he pulled over at his own house. *Harvey you are not thinking clearly, this man is capable of murder. I have seen it with my own eyes. He does not have a conscience! He will kill us!* Shouted Chloe.

Harvey was not listening to a word Chloe had to say. He was full of adrenaline and lacked composure as he got out of the car and ran up the driveway into his house. He first checked the basement and then worked his way up the house looking for Jasper. *Jasper I know you are in here, come and face me you coward. You do not scare me!* Shouted Harvey. After searching the house thoroughly, there was no sign of Jasper. *Harvey the equipment is missing from your office!* Shouted Chloe from downstairs.

Arrrghh I am going to his house! Shouted Harvey as he took a handgun out from a box of shoes from the top of the cupboard. *Harvey why do you have a handgun?* Questioned Chloe. *Because I live in Albawich. Ever wondered how this screwed up town got its name? Albert and witch put both together and you get Albawich.* Explained Harvey. Before getting into his car and speeding off. Leaving Chloe behind. *Harvey please stop!* Shouted Chloe. As Harvey's car faded into the distance.

Harvey approached Jasper's house. Jasper could hear a vehicle approaching. He looked outside and saw the anger on Harvey's face as he stepped out of the car. *Mr Harvey, I have been expecting you.* Jasper whispered. Jasper stepped out of the house to confront Harvey. *Harvey, would you like to come in and have a cup of tea?* Asked Jasper. Harvey pulled out a handgun and fired two shots towards Jasper, hitting the door frame an inch away from Jasper's forehead. *First you tried to kill my friend and then you broke into my house! Come back here and face me you coward!* Shouted

31

Harvey as Jasper ran inside and locked the front door. Harvey approached the house and shot the door lock as he stepped on the porch. He then kicked the door open and was met by the blast of a double barrel shotgun. This sent Harvey flying at least three feet back. *Harvey you silly man look what you have done, you did this to yourself. You are the only one to blame. You should have taken my offer and had a cup of tea with me. Instead, you came to my house guns blazing, I had to rub my eyes to see clearly. I thought I was being approached by Clint Eastwood. There are no heroes in Albawich Harvey, and you are not Clint Eastwood. If you came in a more civil manner, who knows, maybe I would have spared you. You are a smart guy. We could have come to an agreement; you could have traded places with Chloe and lived. But you tried being a hero. Now watch what I do to you.* Threatened Jasper as he approached Harvey.

Surprisingly, Harvey was still alive but losing a lot of blood. Jasper dragged his body to a nearby tree. Jasper kicked Harvey's handgun further away as he dragged Harvey past it. *No no no Harvey, the chance to be a hero ended when you decided that you did not want to have tea with me.* Said Jasper. Jasper walked into the shed and then walked out. Dragging some barbed wire behind him. *Do you want to know my favourite game, Harvey? I will give you two guesses. Oh, sorry you can barely speak. That is my bad Harvey, I am getting old. My eyes sight is not as good as it used to be. So let me tell you. My favourite game is hangman.*

Jasper wrapped the barbed wire around Harvey's neck a couple of times, until it was tightly secure. He attached the other side of the barbed wire around a strong branch on a tree next to the fire pit. Harvey gasped for breath as he choked. *You know me and you, we are not that different. Only you hide behind a false reality, and I am what you see.* Said Jasper as he lifted Harvey over his shoulder. Then threw him down the unlit fire pit, breaking Harvey's neck on impact. *I win!* Shouted Jasper. *Do you want to play another game? Oh, wait you are dead. Never mind I will go find*

Chloe and ask if she would like to have a go at my favourite game. Said Jasper as he walked away from the fire pit.

Chapter Eight

Chloe explored Harvey's house. It was weird and out of character of him to react in the way that he did. He was always of a calm nature, so it was different seeing him display a lot of anger. She had never seen this side of him so she decided to look around his house to see what else she could uncover about him. Everything looked normal, almost too normal. Like a model home in a showroom. It all was put together very thoughtfully.

This was what raised questions in Chloe's mind. *Harvey was always a very busy man, when would he get the time to maintain a house this big to such perfection?* Chloe wondered to herself. There was not even the smallest amount of dust present in the house. Then she entered the basement. The basement was the absolute opposite of the rest of the house. There was so much clutter, cobwebs and dust everywhere. She carefully placed her footing as she looked around the basement. There was nothing but mess. Chloe turned around to go back up the basement stairs. A bookcase on the wall caught here eye. This was the only thing inside the basement that was not covered in dust and cobwebs.

It was very out of place and did not match the rest of the model home theme in the rest of the house. Chloe went closer and examined further. As she removed one of the books from the bookcase labelled '666', she heard something unlock. She stood on the side of the bookcase and pushed it across the wall, revealing a secret room. Chloe entered the room. It was very creepy and dark. The atmosphere was very tense in the room. There were scriptures written in foreign languages scattered all over the floor.

Animal body parts were soaked inside jars and a lot of other bizarre items that must have been used as ingredients for spells.

The walls were covered in newspaper articles of missing people in Albawich. An article about a serial killer named Albert that terrorised Albawich back in the 1800s. Chloe had to cover her mouth as the smell inside the room was revolting. It was almost the same smell that came from Jasper's house. Well, it was now clear that both Jasper and Harvey were into satanic rituals.

There was a book nearby the table. It looked very old; it must have been hundreds of years old. She opened it to reveal many evil spells but the one that had a page marker on it was the 'Wealth Through Knowledge' spell. Next to the spell there were numerous cut-outs of Harvey's awards that he won for his company. It was also now clear that Harvey was involved in the supernatural realm. He got his success from the help of something demonic.

Chloe turned the page and a couple of pages fell out of the book. When Chloe picked them up, she saw that they were a collection of resurrection spells used to bring back the dead. Harvey was involved in something very sinister. He was more than opposite of the person that she thought she knew. This only led to more questions being raised. *Who could Harvey have been trying to bring back from the dead? Can I use this spell to bring back my father?* Chloe realised what she had just said.

It was clear that the room in the basement was affecting her mentally. So she rushed up the stairs slamming the basement door behind her. It was truly shocking what she had uncovered about Harvey in the secret room. Despite all of this, Harvey was still a great person to Chloe so none of this would not affect their friendship. *Maybe I should speak to Harvey, there must be an explanation behind all of this. Surely Harvey would not be involved in such things.* Said Chloe. Trying to convince herself that Harvey was the man that she thought he was.

Chloe was growing concerned for the welfare of Harvey. It had been many hours since he had not returned. Chloe knew that something was not right. She was too afraid to go and look for him. At the same time, she felt that she could not just sit in Harvey's house and wait. It was getting late, so she had to act. She went upstairs and looked in Harvey's wardrobe, there she saw multiple luxury clothing items in various colours. She was never very keen on fashion or the latest trends, but it was clear that Harvey was. Chloe picked out some items and put together a black outfit, which would then allow her to blend into the night, without getting noticed.

Chloe took a knife from the kitchen before leaving the house and setting off towards Jasper's house in the middle of the Albawich woodland. Knowing that the knife would not pose as a threat to Jasper, she only took it to make herself feel safe. Jasper was not her only worry. The Albawich woodland was known to be full of evil entities that lurked day and night. Experiencing this first-hand was even more terrifying than just the thought of it. Chloe walked down the driveway and crossed over to the woodland. As she got deeper into the woodland, she could see the pentagram that she stepped on the other night. Only this time it was glowing with fire. Once again, a bizarre occurrence with such bad weather and damp conditions of the surface.

As Chloe got closer, she could see a group of black hooded people stood around the fire, chanting in a ritualistic manner. She remained calm and managed to sneak past them going unnoticed. She recognised Jasper as one of the people chanting. He was not the hardest person to pick out of the crowd. With his distinct horrific facial features. Knowing the whereabouts of Jasper at this stage of searching for Harvey was a great advantage to Chloe. As this meant that he would not be home. Giving her a small window of opportunity to find Harvey.

She began running until she reached the fallen down tree that she took cover behind, the night she escaped from Jasper's house. This indicated to her that she was running in the right direction. Jasper's house was now visible. Approaching the house, she could see Harvey's car parked up with nobody outside. She then ran towards the front door of the house, noticing the gunshots on the door frame and the door. Pushing through the front door she looked in the lounge. *Harvey? Speak to me, Harvey!* Chloe shouted as she ran up the stairs.

Her heart dropped when the house was empty. She had searched the entire house from top to bottom. She stood panicking staring outside the window at the fire pit. Then realised that there was only one more place to look, the fire pit. The thought of finding Harvey's remains inside the fire pit sent chills down Chloe's spine. She took deep breaths to brace herself for what she was about to see.

There was nothing that she could have done to prepare her for the situation. Tears rolled down Chloe's face as she approached the fire pit, she removed the cover to see the lifeless body of Harvey hanging from the barbed wire. She fell back in shock, crying and panicking. Until she heard multiple footsteps approaching from the distance. It was Jasper and the other Satanists.

Chloe hid on the side of Harvey's car out of their view. Stood in the distance was the tall lady with the white eyes. Staring directly at her. Chloe noticed her and slowly stood up nodding her head left and right, in a plea to the tall white eyed lady not to alert the others of her presence. The white eyed lady ignored Chloe's plea and began to chant. This caught the attention of Jasper and the Satanists. Chloe quickly got into the driver's seat of Harvey's car, luckily the key was still in the ignition. She started the car and sped off in the direction of where she left her own car stranded before the horrific events started to unfold.

Jasper ran towards his truck and set off to pursue Chloe. He could see her taillights in the distance, so he floored the gas pedal to close the distance. Momentarily looking to his side as he loaded bullets into his rifle. He then reached over to the side and took a handgun out of the glove compartment. *You are a brave girl, Chloe. I knew that you would not be able to stop yourself from looking for your friend, but you found me. You thought that I did not see you sneak past me in the woodland? I notice everything Chloe. Even the time you hid inside my laundry basket. I knew that you were there. Killing you then and there would not have been fun. But the officers ruined my plan allowing you to get away. Now I will kill you and have fun doing so.* Jasper psychotically said to himself while attempting to let off a clear shot at Chloe.

This was not possible as the path was narrow, and the branches and other debris kept getting in the way whenever he reached outside the truck. So, Jasper fired a shot through the windscreen so that he could aim and shoot directly in front of him. It was an aimless shot with the intention of shattering the windscreen. Jasper pistol whipped the shattered glass until it had all fallen off completely, continuing to aim towards Chloe's car as he closed the distance on her.

Chloe merged into the road that she had previously been stranded on due to a flood. As she drifted into the road and regained control of her car, her side mirror got blasted off by Jasper. She looked in the rear-view mirror and could see that roughly ten car lengths behind her was Jasper. As he let off more gunshots and closed more of the distance between himself and Chloe. They were both driving at really high speeds, but Jasper was edging closer and closer until he was two car lengths away. Chloe had to think fast to avoid getting shot. So, she made the erratic decision to slam her foot down on the brakes. Causing a disastrous crash, sending Jasper flying out of his seat and over Chloe's car to hit the ground as his body scraped across the road. Chloe's car was totalled. Leaving her windscreen cracked and full of blood.

Chapter Nine

Miraculously she survived and opened the door as her body dropped out of the car. She cried in pain as she dragged her damaged body across to the side of the road. Towards a tree that she used to pull herself up until she was back on her feet. Chloe looked over to the body of Jasper. His face was mostly scraped off including his eye lids. And one of his legs looked to have snapped. Jasper got what he deserved. After all, he was trying to kill Chloe.

At the same time, it was a horrifying sight. She took a deep breath and closed her eyes. Then heard the sound of dragging. When she looked back over at Jasper, he was back on his feet walking towards her with one of his feet scraping across the ground as his leg was broken.

Luckily for Chloe. A car was approaching in the distance. Jasper disappeared into the woodland as Chloe was in too much pain to stand any longer. She collapsed in the road. The car pulled over next to the car wreck. A young couple stepped out of the car and rushed to Chloe. Assuming it was a hit and run situation as Chloe was the only person there and two cars were involved in the accident. *Excuse me lady are you okay? Are you hurt?* Asked the young lady. Chloe was in too much pain to respond. The young couple helped her up and walked her to the back seat of their car and rushed her to safety. Chloe stared out of the back of the car as it drove away. Two white eyes stared back at her from the woodland. Getting smaller and smaller as the car drove further away.

Jasper entered the woods and collapsed shortly before being carried by the white eyed lady. She laid him down on a red pentagram drawn on the ground as the Satanists surrounded him and started chanting. Jasper screamed as the pentagram began to heat up and started glowing before it burst into flames. The white eyed lady started to chant among the Satanists. Jasper's body started to heal, and he grew in size almost like a monster until he was taller than the white eyed lady. His eyes started to glow red as he growled and stood up letting off a huge roar that could be heard throughout the entire town of Albawich. The sound was so terrifying that the locals began to flee from the town of Albawich. And rightly so. They sensed the horror that was coming their way. But they were not ready for the horror that would actually come their way very shortly.

Jasper and the white eyed lady were more powerful than ever as they emerged from the woodland and roamed the streets of Albawich, destroying everything in their path as they searched for Chloe. They brutally killed anybody that they could see. One of the locals ran outside of their house with a Bible and started chanting. The white eyed lady held his head and twisted it until it removed like the lid on a bottle of Pepsi.

Another local ran towards his car with his wife as they threw their suitcases into their car in an attempt to flee. Jasper struck the man with his beastly claw like hand and cut straight through him so deep that you could literally see the view behind him. The white eyed lady dug her nails into the stomach of the man's wife and threw her through a nearby house. She died on impact as her body smashed through the bricks like hot oil on a bar of butter. Hundreds of locals were running through an empty field towards the road that lead out of the town of Albawich. The white eyed lady lifted her hands up into the air and started chanting. Causing the field to become a mass grave.

The hundreds of locals screamed as they fell down into it. But the screams were quickly replaced by silence as the white eyed lady lowered her hands to her side and the soil from the field covered them. Burying them all alive. Rebecca emerged from the woodland. *Minions of Albert! you will repent for the souls that you have hurt. Blinded by Satan in your ways. Death is something every soul shall taste. One day you will have to answer for every sin, evil will never win.* Chanted Rebecca as she stood in front of Jasper and the white eyed lady. *I told you to stay out of my way!* Shouted Jasper as he held her in his hand and crushed her skull. Before throwing her into the woodland. They wreaked havoc as they destroyed Albawich in its entirety. Until it had become a ghost town. Totally abandoned.

The young couple pulled over at their house in a nearby city. And carried Chloe to the front room. The young woman was a nurse and had all of her medical equipment with her. Her boyfriend switched on the television to see if there was anything on that explained the loud horrific roar that they heard. They all watched in shock; every channel was broadcasting aerial footage of Albawich completely destroyed.

It was like a scene from an apocalypse movie. The nurse injected Chloe with a pain killer and bandaged her wounds. *I need to leave; they are looking for me. Lock your doors and stay safe.* Chloe told the young couple. The couple looked at each other and wondered who could be looking for Chloe. None of it made sense to them. It was best for them not to know. So that they could continue to live their lives peacefully.

It was too dangerous for Chloe to stay at the young couple's house as Jasper and the white eyed lady were after her. Having seen what Jasper was capable of, she knew that the complete destruction of Albawich was the work of Jasper and the white eyed lady. They would soon find her. So she decided to stop running as everywhere she went, they would follow and take the lives of more innocent people. Chloe knew what she had to do.

Tired of running. She took the couple's car and drove back to Jasper's house in the Albawich woodland. There were many cars fleeing and people running with their families as they fled the horror of Albawich. It was heart breaking for Chloe to see so many people in distress. To avoid colliding with them, Chloe turned her car into the woodland and drove up to the porch of Jasper's house. Got out of the car and ran into Jasper's house, knowing that he was not there as wherever he went, his truck followed. She got a hold of his rifle and a handgun with a bunch of ammunition clips from above the coat rack.

Surely this would be enough to stop Jasper and the white eyed lady in their tracks, Or not. Either way, there was no other option that Chloe could think of. She felt a sense of guilt for the destruction of Albawich. If she had just let Jasper take her life, then so many people would not have had to flee their homes. At the same time Chloe knew that she was not responsible for Jasper's actions.

Chapter Ten

Chloe spun the car around and floored the gas pedal. She had to become a totally different person as this was a fight for survival. All of the madness drove her from once being a person of civilised character that avoided conflict, into somebody that was willing to do what it took to survive. As she entered the remains of what was left of Albawich. She could not go any further as the roads were blocked by debris of people's houses, smashed cars and dead bodies.

Chloe hung the rifle over her shoulder and held the handgun. A Satanist emerged from the woodland in front of Chloe and started chanting angrily. An emotionless Chloe let off a shot into his leg. Then fired two shots in the air and the rest of the Satanists ran away into the woodland. *JASPER!!!* Shouted Chloe as she followed the trails of wreckage. Knowing that it would lead to Jasper and most likely the white eyed lady. Jasper could not have done all of this alone.

Chloe's screams for Jasper were met by the terrifying chanting of the white eyed lady. Chloe took out a clip of rifle ammo and poured some holy water on it that she had managed to take from Harvey's secret room. After spilling the holy water all over rifle ammo and loading it into the rifle, she let off three bursts of six shots hitting the white eyed lady with every single one of the bullets. Causing her to let out a huge scream in agony as her body dropped to the ground before turning into stone. It was as though she had just locked eyes with Medusa.

Jasper heard the scream of the white eyed lady and ran towards Chloe. Roaring from the top of his lungs, the roar was deafening. Chloe aimed the rifle at him, but it jammed when she pulled the trigger. So she dropped the rifle and poured some of the holy water into the handgun ammo and loaded it into the handgun, before letting off three bursts of six shots at

Jasper. Only two of the three bursts managed to hit Jasper as Chloe loaded the last six rounds into the gun. Jasper barged into Chloe. This sent her flying two feet back without suffering much damage as she landed on a car that broke the fall. The two sets of three shots that Jasper was hit with, weakened him back to his natural state that he was before the spell. He held his hands in front of himself as he noticed that he was no longer a huge beast. His eyes filled with rage.

He walked towards Chloe as she climbed off from the bonnet of the car that she landed on. This was far from over and the real fight for survival was now. He threw a right hook towards Chloe; Chloe pulled her head back dodging the punch causing Jasper to lean in towards her left side as she threw a left hook counter punch followed by a straight right punch to Jasper's face, sending him stumbling back.

He rushed at her again but this time he threw a left uppercut her body, winding her for a couple of seconds until she put both of her hands on his head pulling him down, and delivered a right knee to his face. He then head butted her knocking her to the ground. Sending her handgun sliding under the bonnet of the car. He then jumped on top of her and started to strangle her. She could not push him away. And she was losing her ability to breathe. She quickly spun to the right and elbowed him in the face. Then roundhouse kicked him in the jaw, sending him stumbling backward. Buying her enough time to dive towards the handgun. Turning around just in time to let off the last six rounds into Jasper. Killing him instantly as his body dropped on top of Chloe.

Chloe pushed the dead weight away from herself. The last few days were more than she bargained for. She stood up from the ground and got back into the car she took from the young couple. And drove through the woodland. A police car dropped from the top of the tree, blocking Chloe's path. This was the car that Jasper had lifted into the trees from his earlier encounter with the two police officers. Chloe turned the car around and entered a dirt road that seemed to lead away from Albawich as the other routes out of Albawich were blocked off. There was a huge creepy abandoned building in the distance. It looked like it was something straight out of a Dracula movie. She pulled over to have a look. As she stepped out of the car she walked towards the abandoned mansion.

There was some smoke coming from the shed. It must have recently been burnt down. Towering above her was the huge creepy abandoned mansion. With the words 'Albert Mansion' engraved above the entrance doors. An eerie feeling of being watched came over Chloe. Her attention went towards one of the windows upstairs. A child, a man and a women were all stood staring at her. The man had a creepy smile. It curved from one earlobe to the other. Chloe turned around in terror and got back into the car before speeding away.

Chloe looked in her rear-view mirror. She could see Albawich getting smaller and smaller. This filled her with comfort knowing that she had finally escaped the horror that she was stuck in the middle of. Not long after she had reached her apartment. A view that she had not been this happy to see before. She smiled as she could see the sun rising from the horizon. She parked her car and entered the building. As she ran up the stairs, she could see people walking out of a room that blasted out music momentarily before the door shut behind them.

Another party, if only these people knew how lucky they were, just minding their business enjoying themselves with no demons to bother them. Joked Chloe as she passed by the room. After running up a few more floors, Chloe approached her apartment and opened the door. The calm atmosphere ended abruptly. Her room was completely vandalised. Demonic symbols were drawn all over the walls. The photos of herself and her friends were all vandalised. Chloe left her apartment in fear and exited the

45

building before running into her car and speeding away. She had no where else to go. They had found where she lived and got there before her. Chloe could not think of who it could be that vandalised her apartment. It could not have been Jasper or the white eyed lady, as she watched them both die in front of her. Her horrors were clearly not over yet. She felt that every time she would celebrate surviving the horrors of Albawich, she would find herself in the middle of another creepy situation.

Chapter Eleven

Chloe decided that it would be a good idea to drive to her Aunt Margaret's house. Margaret raised Chloe after her father died. She was like a mother to her. She had no children of her own, neither had she ever been married. Chloe adopted her kind nature from her Aunt Margaret. It was a two-hour journey from Chloe's apartment. Chloe stopped at a petrol station nearby to buy some snacks and fill the car up with fuel. As she stepped out of the car she looked up at the sky. In the distance she could see a dark cloud heading in her direction. She did not want to get stranded because of another flood.

As she remembered the horror that she had faced the last time she was stranded. Chloe hurried into the store after filling the fuel into her car. She paid for the fuel and on the fuel station television she could see the weather was forecast to bring potential floods. She ran to the car and sped towards her Aunt Margaret's house. The young lady that the car belonged to conveniently had left her trench coat hung on the back of the seat. Chloe wore it in order to cover up her wounds and ruined clothes. She turned the rear-view mirror towards herself and practiced happy smiles.

So that she could avoid any suspicion of anything being wrong when she would meet her Aunt Margaret. She approached the house, and this bought back many memories. Memories of the times when she used to come back from college and Aunt Margaret would have fresh food and dessert on the table ready for her to dig into. Chloe had never met her mother. But she was convinced that her Aunt Margaret's love was the closest thing to what a mother's love would be like.

As she pulled on to the drive. Aunt Margaret came outside the front door. *Oh, good heavens Chloe, I did not know that you were coming. I would have made you a lovely feast.* Said Aunt Margaret as she hugged Chloe. As soon as Chloe Stepped out of the car. *Aunt Margaret I thought I would surprise you.* Said Chloe. *Well, you have certainly surprised me please come in. I have not seen you in a while.* Said Aunt Margaret. *That is why I am going to be stopping over with you for a while, to make up for all of the time we have been apart.* Said Chloe. *In that case let me show you to your room. It is just as you left it. Mind you, it has only been a couple of months since you last stayed.* Said Aunt Margaret as she left Chloe in her bedroom, allowing her to settle in. Chloe laid back on the bed and removed her trench coat before changing into some clean clothes. She freshened up and went downstairs. *I am heading out sweetie I got plans with some friends. I will be back tonight there is some vegetable soup and bread rolls in the kitchen. Help yourself.* Said Aunt Margaret as she headed out.

Chloe walked into the front room and sat at the computer. Now was the time for her to write the news article, but something did not feel right. The heavy rain and thunder had now moved in. As the wind howled creating an eerie atmosphere. Chloe heard the floorboards creaking upstairs and then heard a door being opened and then it slammed shut.

Aunt Margaret is that you? Did you forget something? Asked Chloe as she slowly stepped out of the front room. Chloe did not want to go up the stairs. She had experienced many horrors over the last few days. At the same time her strong will did not allow her to sit and wait for her Aunt Margaret to eventually return. She slowly made her way upstairs. *Hello, Aunt Margaret.* Chloe said once again after hearing more footsteps. She opened the door to the room where the sounds were coming from. And there was nobody there. *It is probably the heavy winds causing the house to rattle.* Said Chloe as she tried to justify the sounds that came from one of the rooms upstairs.

Aunt Margaret could return at any time. And Chloe needed to take a shower as her body was still unwashed since the night she stayed at Harvey's house. She walked into her bedroom and looked inside the wardrobe. Not long before she took some clean clothes from the wardrobe and got into the shower. After she had completed her shower she stared into the mirror, to her surprise there was no longer any scars on her back. The '666' sign had completely disappeared from her back with no outlines or traces of it ever being on her back. Chloe felt cleansed as she stepped out of the shower. She dried herself down and got dressed.

When she walked into her room, she looked in the mirror whilst drying and brushing her hair. And then she noticed a part of her mattress pushed down as if somebody was sat on her bed. This was getting too much for Chloe. As there was no reduction in the scary experiences that she was having. She thought that she was safe in Aunt Margaret's house. This was clearly not the case.

Chloe screamed and rushed down the stairs. Running out of the front door. A shadowy figure could be seen staring at her from one of the windows upstairs. Chloe was too frightened to look back. She got in the car and drove a couple of minutes away. Where she stopped the car at a reservoir. Her belly rumbled as she was starving. She could see a fish and chips van nearby. She decided to get some and then sat peacefully eating whilst looking at the beautiful nature that surrounded the reservoir.

Excuse me miss, are you okay? Asked a man that stopped his car besides Chloe's car. *Yes, why wouldn't I be?* Responded Chloe. *I do not remember the last time I saw somebody parked there, especially whilst eating. Anyways, suit yourself.* Said the man before driving away. Chloe turned around and the reservoir was not what she was looking at before. It was like it had transformed. What she was looking at was a huge sewer littered with rats and surrounded by overgrown weeping trees. The smell made Chloe barf. She could not eat anymore of her food, so she threw it into a bin nearby. It was now clear that she was being haunted. This was the only explanation for the recent events she had experienced.

It was late evening, Chloe returned to her aunt Margaret's house. Nobody was home. Something passed by the window upstairs as Chloe entered the house. The electricity was gone so the lights were not working. Chloe walked to the kitchen and found a lighter, remembering that there was a candle in the front room. Chloe entered the front room and approached the candle. Something nudged into her. This freaked Chloe out. She ran to the candle and quickly lit it. And quickly looked around, there was nobody there. Chloe was too scared to leave the room, so she sat in the front room. The electricity came back on. To her comfort aunt Margaret had also just arrived.

Aunt Margaret walked into the front room to see Chloe holding a candle. *Haha why are you sat here holding a lit candle with the light on? Come help me put the shopping away.* Laughed aunt Margaret. Chloe helped Aunt Margaret put the shopping away. The atmosphere in the house had returned to a peaceful one. Chloe made herself and Aunt Margaret a cup of tea as they sat in the front room watching serial killer documentaries. Chloe used to love watching them. But with her recent experiences watching people being murdered, Chloe did not enjoy watching the documentaries one bit.

She could not tell Aunt Margaret this as she would notice that something was terribly wrong. Both ladies were starting to fall asleep. Until Aunt Margaret switched off the television. *Come on sweetie wake up, your bed is much comfier that the sofa that you are sleeping on. Come on get up and go to your room Chloe before you get a neckache by resting you head on the arm rest.* Said Aunt Margaret. They both went to bed as it got really late. Chloe woke up middle of the night and could hear the sounds of whispering. She looked around the room slowly and could not see anything. But when she looked besides herself, somebody was laying down with their back facing her. *Aunt Margaret is that you?*

Asked Chloe. Hoping that this was her Aunt Margaret. Chloe leaned over and saw the disfigured face of the thing laying next to her. And screamed then ran into the hallway. Before entering her aunties room. *Chloe why do you look so scared.* Asked aunt Margaret. *There is something in my room, this house is haunted. You do not live alone!* Shouted Chloe.

Aunt Margaret then stood up at the front of her bed and walked into the hallway as Chloe stayed sat frozen in terror. A couple of minutes passed by, and Aunt Margaret returned. *Oh, Chloe what have you done? My house was peaceful until you came here. There was nothing but peace and holiness in this house until you bought evil along with you. Just like your father, you bring trouble with you! Leave at once!* Shouted Aunt Margaret in anger. Chloe ran down the stairs and walked out of the house. As she opened the car door, she looked back and saw the thing from her bed with the disfigured face stood behind Aunt Margaret. *Aunt Margaret!* Shouted Chloe as the front door slammed shut. Followed by the screams of Aunt Margaret and a splatter of blood covered the glass surrounding the door. Chloe started the car and sped off back toward Albawich.

Chapter Twelve

She thought that Albawich was in her past. But she had been riddled by hauntings ever since she first entered Albawich. Chloe knew that something evil still lurked within the town. She had to put an end to all of this. It was killing innocent people and haunting her no matter where she was. Her life was becoming unbearable. She turned onto the dirt road and approached the Albert mansion before parking up. She stared at the shed and then stared at the mansion.

She started having flashbacks of the news articles that she had read in Harvey's secret room about the serial killer named Albert, that terrorised the town of Albawich during the 1800s. It was clear that Albert's shed was not set on fire for no reason. And maybe if his mansion burnt down then this would put an end to all of the madness. A wild theory this was. But it was the only one. Her life was falling apart, so she took her chances with deciding to follow through with her plan to burn down Albert's mansion.

As she drove down the dirt path her car emerged from the woodland. And right in front of her stood the house of Jasper. Chloe parked up near the shed. She walked into the shed and saw huge containers of fuel. She rolled two of them towards her car and lifted them one at a time before putting them in the boot. She then went to Jasper's house to find some matches or even a lighter. She stepped into the kitchen and searched all of the cupboards. She had no luck finding a lighter or matches.

She went upstairs and looked through a bedside cabinet and found a lighter. She clicked the button to see if it was in working order, which it was. Then Chloe rushed down the stairs and out on to the porch. To her surprise she could hear the sounds of chanting. She fell back in horror as she saw Jasper emerging from the woods with the few Satanists that ran into the woods. She had a flashback of when she let off two shots into the air allowing them to get away from her. Letting them live was a grave mistake made by Chloe. As they most definitely got together and performed a resurrection ritual on Jasper to bring him back to life.

By the time she gathered herself and stood up, it was too late. Jasper and the Satanists were too close for Chloe to get away. They held her arms as Jasper head butted her out of consciousness. Jasper and the Satanists carried Chloe's unconscious body deep into the woodland. Chloe started to gain consciousness and woke up facing the white eyed lady.

The white eyed lady strangled Chloe and lifted her body into the air while she paced towards the pentagram. The white eyed lady let go of Chloe once she was directly above the pentagram. Snapping both of her legs on impact. She screamed in pain as the white eyed witch reached down to Chloe's chest ripping her heart out with her bare hands. Squeezing it whilst the blood poured all over her face. Chloe closed her eyes. Never to wake up ever again. Jasper roared as the pentagram burst into flames around Chloe's lifeless body.

It was not Albert's mansion that was the source of evil it was the land on which Albawich sat. The land absorbed the unspeakable evil things that happened on top of it. For over two hundred years the trees witnessed countless innocent lives being taken in the most brutal ways. The ground laid as a venue for such events. Even the sky looked down upon the evil brutalities that took place in Albawich.

Albawich became the most unholy land on the earth. Where evil would always win. The government knew this, that's why the public transport services never served return tickets to Albawich. Only one-way tickets. Because they knew that whoever enters Albawich never leaves, even after they die. Their soul would wonder the town of Albawich for eternity.

The evil's very own breeding ground. Waiting for the next innocent soul to visit its soul hungry land that has been starving for over two hundred years. Not once has its hunger been content with the number of souls that it has devoured.

The following morning, a missing persons report had been filed. And posters of Chloe were hung up around the town of Albawich. News companies had started going on air to report the disappearance of Chloe. One of them saying. *Concerns are growing for the welfare of the news reporter named Chloe Slater. She was last seen a couple of days ago in the woodland area of Albawich. The bizarre thing that left investigators confused was that Chloe Slaters apartment was full of demonic symbols that suggest that she was involved in dark arts. The general public are being advised by the authorities to stay away from Chloe Slater. Do not approach her, call the police and get yourself to safety. And lastly, the authorities have advised to lock your doors and windows before going to bed. Thank you for tuning into Albawich Today. Harvey Adams.*